LISA
Likes Ice-skating

AuthorHouse™ UK
1663 Liberty Drive
Bloomington, IN 47403 USA
www.authorhouse.co.uk
UK TFN: 0800 0148641 (Toll Free inside the UK)
UK Local: 02036 956322 (+44 20 3695 6322 from outside the UK)

This book is printed on acid-free paper.

ISBN: 978-1-6655-9600-8 (sc)
ISBN: 978-1-6655-9601-5 (e)

Print information available on the last page.

Published by AuthorHouse 01/18/2022

authorHOUSE®

LISA
Likes Ice-skating

BRENDAH GAINE

Foreword

These three stories written by Brendah Gaine, of children acting as carers, in a family struggling with difficulties, demonstrates the importance of a kind, compassionate and reassuring adult to whom the child can turn for help. The stories offer a creative means of helping to open up discussion, giving the child an opportunity to identify with the characters. Young carers often speak about the sense of their fear, worry and responsibility as well as isolation from peers. Additionally, in one of the stories there is mention of the impact on school work. All this shows how important it is to give a voice to the child. In each story there is a child protection element and therefore a statutory responsibility to refer to the relevant agency so that these issues can be addressed first and foremost. In one of the stories the teacher acknowledges the courage of the child in asking for help. The boy has to overcome his fear of something calamitous happening for speaking up. The role of the adult is a skilled, delicate and patient one and the notes at the end of the stories emphasise the importance of the discussions. Creative ideas and mindfulness exercises are suggested to help the child process and overcome the trauma of shouldering the family difficulties and these ideas are suggested with the child alongside the trusted adult. In one of the stories there is a delightful example of support and a fun outing for the whole family and this reassurance is another example of the weight of responsibility being lifted from the child's shoulders. Brendah offers an insight born out of many years of professional practice, including teaching and work with children and families through psychotherapy. The stories are grounded in authenticity and truth and would be a welcome and valuable additional resource in a variety of settings including a therapeutic one.

Helen Trevor Davies BA, CQSW (Certificate of Social Work) Goldsmiths
Retired Social Worker, Child and Adolescent Mental Health Service, Enfield
Former Child Protection Officer, NSPCC

Acknowledgements

My thanks go to the families who helped me to listen to their struggles and together we worked on solutions to learn to cope both emotionally and practically. I also want to thank Helen Trevor Davies for her carefully worded foreword. As always I thank David and Megan for supporting me with the technological hurdles.

Lisa lives with her Mum and two brothers in a small two-bedroom flat in a big city. She shares a room with her Mum and her two brothers share the other bedroom. Dad left just after her younger brother Dodi was born and although he promised to be back he hasn't returned and nobody knows where he is. Lisa feels sad, angry and confused about her dad because he left six years ago now. Jack, her other brother, is 8 and she is just 10 years old. She doesn't have time to go outside to play because on Mum's bad days she has to make sure that the boys have something to eat after school; that they wash and get into pyjamas early so that she can do homework before checking on how Mum is.

She loves her brothers but sometimes they can be a pain and Lisa feels angry with them when they are silly. Dodi was the most difficult and runs off in the opposite direction or hides away when she calls them for tea. Jack can be very cheeky and says he's big enough to come in when he's ready. Especially in the summer, they say it's too early to have to wash and get ready for bed. She bribes them by saying "Okay, you can watch telly until half past seven." Their bed-time is usually seven o'clock.

Sometimes mum stays in bed for days and Lisa has to do all the household chores as well as giving more attention to her brothers.

"Does anyone else have to do all this?" Lisa thinks to herself but never says it to anyone. Lisa finds that mostly she has to keep her eye on her mum taking her tablets. If she doesn't do that mum forgets and then she feels glum and just pulls the blanket over her head and won't speak to anyone. She has, before now, taken too many tablets and Lisa was not able to wake her. This is scary.

She has, at those times, thought her mum had died. She knows that she has to call for an ambulance and while she waits for them to come she is very scared. Sometimes the boys don't even know that mum has to go to hospital again because they are asleep or watching telly. Its only when Dodi asks "Where's mum?" that she has to tell them she's in hospital but will soon be out.

At times like this their next door neighbour, Mrs Cooper, stays with them until mum gets home again. Mrs Cooper is very kind and understands how scared Lisa feels. She can talk to Mrs Cooper about how she feels. Lisa thinks that Mrs Cooper must have been a social worker when she was younger because she always knows what do to and who to talk to. She tells Lisa "I'll have to phone Social Services again so that the social worker can come to see how you all are. I will always be there for you, Jack and Dodi but I must tell the Social."

Lisa is worried that they will have to go into Care with other families when her mum is not well. It happened a few times before when they were split up and sent to different people. Mum stayed in hospital a long time then. Lisa didn't like that and is pleased that Mrs Cooper helps out. It's strange, but when Mrs Cooper asked her how she was feeling, Lisa said, "You know what I'd like to do, Mrs Cooper? I'd like to be like that ice skater on the telly who glides along without a care in the world."

Mrs Cooper said, "I know you have lots of worries when your mum is not well and when your brothers need help. But if you like to ice-skate, why don't we all go to the ice rink next week. We can go as spectators to watch then it isn't too expensive. You can really see what it's like and decide when you want to have a go."

"I'd really like that, Mrs Cooper."

"I'll ask your Mum," said Mrs Cooper.

"I'll also ask her," said Lisa

Well, her wish came true very soon after that. Mrs Cooper and Mum organised the outing to the Ice Skating rink. They all went along and mum was happy to see Lisa enjoying herself. Lisa thought, "Why can't it always be like this?" She didn't say anything but the next time she spoke to Mrs Cooper she told her how happy she was to go to the ice rink.

An even bigger surprise was in store for Lisa. Her birthday was coming up soon and mum had organised a Skating party with the family and her best friend Molly. It was fun because everyone had a go on the ice rink. Molly was good at skating so she helped Lisa to stay balanced. What a surprise when Lisa found that she was brave enough to have a go on her own. She got confident very quickly. Even Mrs Cooper and mum had a go and she didn't have to worry about her brothers because they kept an eye on them.

"I wish we could always be so happy," thought Lisa. But she knew that the next time that mum was unwell she would have to do what she could to look after her. It was good to know that Mrs Cooper was there to help too. Lisa didn't feel so alone.

She could always dream about being an ice skater now she knew she could do it.

"Good old Mrs Cooper," Lisa thought as she drifted off to sleep that birthday night.

Note for Adults:

This story can also be used to describe loss of childhood as the young carer has to take on the responsibility of caring for the family in the absence of responsible parents.

Points for discussion:

- How did Lisa express her feelings?

- Does it help to talk to an adult or a friend?

- What would you do if you were in Lisa's place/situation?

- What thoughts and feelings did you have when you read the story?

- Did you like it or did you disagree with the help that the Mrs Cooper gave to Lisa?

- What would you like to do now that you have found out about a young carer like Lisa?

Printed in the United States
by Baker & Taylor Publisher Services